To Die a Lonely Death

By

Jill S. Adams

To everyone captivated by the mysterious charm and enigmatic allure of Jazz-age New Orleans.

1939 did not leave quietly when the new year arrived at Bones' music club. No; the sound of jazz, swing, and jive filled the room throughout the evening until, at midnight, finally exhausted and with one last gasp, the raucous celebration was handed over to the more youthful and energetic 1940, and the festivities continued well into the morning.

1

The evening had been a tremendous success. Bones and his partner Aloha were optimistic about the prospects of the coming year as the last of the evening's revelers departed. The club had been partially destroyed by a fire earlier in the year and, although it had reopened a few weeks later, it now felt officially back to normal, the new year promising.

    The look of the club, more a restoration than a transformation, reflected its original appearance. The only new addition was a huge sign that covered the wall over the main entrance. The brightly colored neon depicted a reclining skeleton playing a clarinet, emitting musical notes that blinked on and off in rhythmic formation.

    Aloha was making the relentless back and forth from the tables to the kitchen, clearing what seemed to be an endless parade of glassware. She rounded up the mutinous stragglers hiding throughout the club, bringing them to join the others already awaiting a dip in a sink full of hot dishwater.

Bones stood nearby, mop in hand. "Aloha, let's call it quits for tonight. We can come back and finish up tomorrow."

Aloha looked around the club. Fastidious by nature, she hated to leave anything undone, but they were both totally spent from the night's work, and it was nearly dawn.

She nodded at Bones. "Let me wipe down these tables and I'll be ready to go."

A few minutes later, they were locking the club's front door and turning to walk the two blocks up Rampart Street where Bones had to park the car on the holiday eve. They walked arm in arm, content but exhausted, until they were abruptly stopped by a prone figure at their feet. A man was propped against the long corner window of the hardware store where a narrow alley met Rampart Street. "Here's one that's had a little too much New Year's Eve. Looks like he's out cold." Aloha grinned.

Bones took a step back, then knelt down for a closer look. The man was well dressed, wearing a silver-gray suit cut from an expensive fabric. His head rested against the shop window, the mouth partially open, the eyes staring blankly ahead. They were the unique color of cornflower blue and gave off an unusual glow in the early light.

Bones gave the man a nudge and he promptly fell forward, revealing a trickle of crimson seeping out from under the silver suit jacket. Bones stepped back again. "Aloha, this ain't no overindulging partygoer. Go back to the club and call the police, now..."

Aloha glanced from Bones to the prone stranger, barely hesitating before she ran back to the music club.

2

Bones shifted his weight back and forth from foot to foot, then walked in a circle, escaping the chill in the air as he waited for Aloha's return. The streets were deserted. Even the hardiest partygoers had gone home or at least found a warm place indoors. He was alone with the dead man, and he bent over to take a closer look. Those bright eyes, the thin mustache, the well-tailored suit. He turned to see Aloha coming toward him. She was assuring him the police were on their way just as he heard the distant sirens.

An ambulance arrived accompanied by two patrol cars, out of the first of which emerged Lieutenant Kevin O'Connor. He nodded to Bones and Aloha as he strode past them to approach the body. He took a few minutes to observe, then located and examined a pair of chest wounds. Finally, he padded the suit pockets in an effort to obtain any identification. He extricated a single card from a breast pocket. He rose to his feet, allowing the forensic team to begin its work. He returned to Bones and Aloha who were huddling together on the pavement.

"Nice to see you both again, despite the circumstances." O'Connor had met the couple earlier in the year in connection with the arson at the club. "Talk to me about finding this guy."

Bones reiterated the details of the time since they closed the club.

"Ever seen him before? Was he in the club tonight?"

"No," Bones replied. Aloha quickly echoed his response. "Of course, we were really busy; a lot of folks were in and out of the place all night long."

Aloha spoke up. "But I don't remember seeing him at all." She glanced at Bones, who nodded in agreement.

"I found this in his pocket." O'Connor produced the card he had taken from the body. The couple looked at the card, then back at the Lieutenant. It was the business card of detective Jack Dawson, a friend of both the duo and Lieutenant O'Conner.

"Was Jack in the club last night?" the Lieutenant inquired.

"He was in, but he left early. Long before the new year," Bones answered.

"This card is all I found on the body, no identification. Maybe Jack ran into him somewhere." O'Connor turned as a stretcher was wheeled to the ambulance.

"Looks like two bullet wounds. Been dead a few hours," a medical attendant shouted at the Lieutenant. "We'll know more when we get him on the table".

O'Connor waved the forensics team off. He rubbed his hand across his forehead as a smirk formed on his mouth. Shots fired on New Year's Eve, he thought. No one would even notice.

"Want me to call Jack?" Bones looked at the lieutenant.

O'Connor thought for a moment. "No, you two go on home and get some rest. I'll call on Jack."

The couple turned and walked hand in hand to their car, grateful to finally be headed home.

3

Jack Dawson had spent the greater part of New Year's Eve at Velma's boarding house, where he retained rooms despite his growing business and improved financial status. He visited his friends Bones and Aloha at their music club on Rampart Street before returning to Velma's to ring in the new year. Velma's two sons had both gotten leave from the military, and her husband was home from his cross-country driving job for the holiday. Jack, being almost a third son to Velma, joined in the family's celebrations. Careful not to overindulge, he was looking forward to a restful, lazy New Year's Day.

So it was with weary reluctance that he rose to answer the knock at his door early in the morning. Expecting a bright-eyed Velma with a tray of beignets and coffee, he was surprised to see Kevin O'Connor standing in the doorway.

"Kevin," Jack stepped back rubbing his eyes as the policeman entered. "What brings you here on the first day of the year?"

The Lieutenant carefully detailed the night's events as they sat at Jack's kitchen table.

"Well,", Jack began deliberately. "You have a well-dressed, blue-eyed corpse with two slugs in his chest."

"A corpse with no identification, just your business card in his pocket!"

"Kevin, you know my cards are all over town. He could have picked one up anywhere."

"I know Jack, but if you have seen the guy, it could move us closer to finding out who he is…"

Jack knew what was being asked, and he moved to the bedroom and began dressing.

"Okay, Kevin. Take me down to the morgue."

4

Jack's visit to the morgue failed to yield any new information. He neither recognized nor remembered the thin figure now lying peacefully on the metal table. He joined Lieutenant O'Connor for a coffee in the coroner's office.

"Jack, do me a favor. Somebody's got to know this guy. Someone knows something about him. I'm going to take a photo around to some of the local businesses. You think you could show one around some of the clubs you go to?" He handed Jack a picture of the dead man.

Not particularly unpleasant for a coroner's photograph, thought Jack. Well, he wasn't busy at the office during the holidays, and it would be easy enough to help Kevin and the police department, so he agreed to do what he could.

"He might have been an out-of-towner, so hotels may be a good start." Jack looked at Kevin.

"That's where I'm headed after I take you home."

Jack sat at the kitchen table in his room at Velma's and pulled the picture of the dead man out of his suit jacket. He studied the narrow face with the thin mustache. The closed eyelids hid the penetrating blue eyes, but the photo would be usable tomorrow as he made his rounds to clubs, most of which would be closed on New Year's Day. For now, he'd head to Bones' music club to hear what Bones and Aloha had to say about the previous evening.

He parked next to Bones' Ford sedan behind the club and knocked on the rear door. It was quickly answered by Aloha, wiping her hands with a dish towel.

"Jack, come on in." She stepped back, giving him room to enter. "Guess you talked to the Lieutenant already about last night. We couldn't sleep so we came back here early to clean up. Almost done now. I was just heating up some crab soup for Bones and me. Wanna try some?"

Jack nodded his assent with a smile, never able to resist Aloha's cooking. He took a seat at the bar, and she soon returned with the hot bowl. "That poor man. Terrible thing to find him like that. Did you know him, Jack? The Lieutenant said he had your card."

"No, I never saw him."

"Well, he wasn't in the club. At least we don't remember seeing him. I guess it's nothing to do with us then." She brightened for a moment, looking down at the steaming soup. "New year, new recipe. You'll like it."

She returned to the kitchen just as Bones emerged from the storeroom with an armful of liquor bottles. He deposited them behind the bar and took a seat next to Jack. Aloha brought him an aromatic bowl, then retreated to the kitchen.

Bones greeted Jack, then lowered his voice and spoke urgently. "Jack, we gotta talk. I mean, I think I know the guy...the dead guy."

Jack froze, spoon in hand.

"I don't mean I knew him," Bones continued. "But I recognized him."

"Did you say anything to Lieutenant O'Conner?"

"No." Bones shook his head. "I didn't even tell Aloha. I'm pretty darn sure, but on the off chance I'm wrong, I don't want to worry her, after what happened last year with the fire, you know, Jack."

Jack felt a sense of responsibility for what had befallen his friends since the fire had been a warning to him to back off a case.

"How do you know the guy?"

Bones took a deep breath before responding. "When I was playing with bands back in New York, there were always a lot of small-time agents trying to get musicians to sign dubious contracts. You had to really watch who you got involved with, and this guy was one of the shadiest. He'd double-deal his clients, book non-existent gigs, all kinds of underhanded stuff. To make things worse, he was known to deal some pretty hardcore drugs, gettin' guys hooked and dependent on him. If you were smart you stayed away from him. You know, we did our share of drinkin' and smokin' that jazz cabbage, but I saw too many guys brought down on that heavy stuff."

"You know him by name?" Jack asked.

"Everyone called him Frankie, no last name. I would swear it's the same guy. Those blue eyes."

"What would he be doing here in New Orleans?"

"I have no idea, Jack. He must have made a lot of enemies over the years, but I never heard of him operating around here."

"You've got to tell O'Conner and Aloha. She can take it."

Bones looked toward the kitchen where Aloha was bustling about placing glassware in the cupboards.

"I will."

Jack sat back in thought. Frankie. Not much help perhaps, but a start at least. He picked up his spoon and delved into the flavorful broth.

Jack began the following morning by showing the victim's picture at cafes and bars opening for the lunch trade. He started in the Quarter, close to where the body had been found, but was met with negative responses from everyone in the service trades.
He eventually worked his way across Canal Street and on to St. Charles. Knowing the victim was a natty dresser, he stopped into Meyer the Hatter on the chance the man had made a purchase at the well-known shop, but neither Pete nor anyone on his staff recognized the man in the picture.

Jack moved further down St. Charles, enjoying the sliver of sunlight emerging from behind a sky full of clouds. He paused in front of The Anchorage, a neighborhood bar run by Salty Monroe, and known by locals as Salty's Place.

Salty was a Navy veteran, something he was extremely proud of, and he was usually found behind the bar, or in the tiny kitchen, sporting a stained apron over a white undershirt with the sleeves rolled up.

The bar itself was a hodgepodge of photographs and souvenirs from Salty's life at sea, randomly arranged and covered in a layer of dust. It would be just another "beer joint", popular with locals interested in listening to a boxing match on the radio or grabbing a quick shot on the way home from work, but Salty had a star attraction: the beautiful chanteuse, Lita Vendome.

Lita had been married to a notorious gambler who had been killed in an altercation with a competitor a few years before. As a friend of her husband, and himself besotted with Lita, Salty stepped in, providing Lita with a place to stay and a venue for talent. Lita was grateful for the opportunity and performed five nights a week, packing in the crowds and filling the coffers for Salty as he worshipped from afar. Lita's looks and voice could have taken her to any stage in New Orleans and beyond, but if she harbored any aspirations of further fame, she kept them well hidden. So, the arrangement worked for both Lita, who lacked for nothing and remained in the spotlight she loved, and Salty who reaped the financial rewards while being close to his muse.

The Anchorage sat back from the street in an older stone building with large windows and a high arched entrance way. Jack reached for the heavy door, pausing momentarily to peruse the wooden signboard outside that depicted the stunning Lita in a glittery gown and a list of her performance days and times. Everyone in town seemed to know Lita and Salty, and Jack was no exception. He swung the door open, spreading light into the dark interior. Salty was behind the bar and turned, putting a hand to his brow to shield his eyes from the glare. It only took a second for him to discern the silhouette, and he broke into a wide grin.

"Jack Dawson. Long time no see." Salty reached out with a strong handshake.

Two women stood at the far end of the bar, looking over a packet of sheet music. Then both looked up, Lita's shining black hair grazing her shoulders. Her porcelain skin and full lips, accented in crimson, only served to enhance her beauty.

"Jack," she smiled. She was accompanied by her good friend, Nettie Myles, herself an accomplished singer. Nettie had stopped performing after she married a jazz drummer and had promptly become the mother of four boys. "I'm putting some new songs into my routine." Lita glanced down at the music. "You should come see the show sometime, Jack. What brings you here at this time of day?"

Jack explained the reason for his visit and reached into his pocket to produce the picture of the dead man.

Salty took a long look, inhaled deeply, and closed his eyes. He turned the picture over and placed it face down on the bar.

"No," he said. "He's not one of our customers."

Nettie lifted the picture at one edge and looked underneath like a poker player examining her cards. She slowly turned it over. Looking over Nettie's shoulder,

Lita let out a gasp, but they both shook their heads, denying any recognition of the victim.

Jack took a chance and brought up the name Frankie. Lita turned away and all three denied knowing any customer that went by that name. Jack thanked them while retrieving the photograph and was moving towards the entrance when Salty called him aside.

"Don't think twice about how Lita reacted to that picture. She's real sensitive, and the photo of a dead man upset her. Some people are like that, you know."

Jack assured him that he had made no inference from Lita's behavior, but once outside he rethought it. Her reaction was a bit unusual, but was there anything suspicious about it? Was she shocked because she recognized the man? But if she did, why not say so? Jack walked out to the car. He had one more stop to make at Malcolm's Barber Shop before he headed back to the office.

6

Known to be well dressed and well groomed, it wasn't surprising that Jack made regular visits to Malcolm's Barber Shop on Chartres Street. He pushed open the door, ringing the little bell that dangled above the doorway that alerted Malcolm to incoming customers. Sweeping up remnants of his previous client's trim, Malcolm motioned Jack to a chair. As he began, Jack brought out the picture and mentioned the name Frankie, but Malcolm didn't recall seeing the man. He did remark on the victim's meticulous haircut.

"A very nice cut indeed. Precise, up-to-date, stylish. But, sorry to say, not my work."

Twenty minutes later, Jack was trotting up the stairs to his second-floor office, wondering if anyone at all had seen Frankie and knew what he was doing in New Orleans.

7

He rounded the corner at the top of the stairs, seeing the light behind the beveled glass of his office door that ensured Emily Garver, his secretary, was diligently attending to her duties. He had hired Mrs. Garver when paperwork and phone requests for his services had multiplied after his well-publicized case last spring. She had been a secretary for the police department and came highly recommended by Lieutenant O'Connor. Her extreme efficiency had proven invaluable, and Jack was grateful for her able assistance.

He opened the office door and Emily looked up. She had been examining a paper she had pulled from a file on her desk as she lifted her eyeglasses from the bridge of her nose, which allowed them to dangle from the chain around her neck. Her short hair was dark and beginning to be threatened with strands of gray. She wore a neat skirt and sweater set and rubber-soled shoes that enabled her to move quickly and silently around the office.

"Mr. Dawson." She addressed him formally when clients were present. "There's a couple in your office. They want to speak with you about the body that was found on New Year's Day."

Emily had left the door ajar, and Jack glanced into the inner office. A heavy man sat slouched in an office chair with a tall angular woman standing beside him. The man struggled to his feet as Jack entered, extending a plump hand.

"Mr. Dawson, I'm Stanley Gerard, and I want you to find out who killed my brother Frank."

Jack observed the man in front of him. He was cheaply dressed with a poorly knotted tie that he had loosened around his neck. His fair hair had been cut extremely short; his face pudgy with a dimpled double chin. He seemed to bear no resemblance to the dead man until he looked directly at Jack with the identical penetrating blue eyes.

"Oh, I know what you're thinking." Stan chuckled. "Frankie and I don't look like brothers. Yeah, he was more Errol Flynn, and I guess I'm more Allen Hale." He patted his stomach and laughed again. "And," he nodded toward the woman at his side, "this is my wife, Beatrice. Everybody calls her Bix."

The lanky Mrs. Gerard wore a polka dot dress with a felt hat perched on her head covered with tiny bunches of cherries. Her short blonde hair remained stiff and motionless as she leaned forward to shake Jack's hand. Her face revealed no emotion, and she remained stoic as her husband continued speaking.

"This will really throw you." Stan smiled at Jack. "My Bix and Frankie's wife Bunny are sisters. Yep, we're brothers who married sisters. How do you like that?"

Jack managed a wry smile. "Sit down, both of you, please. Let's start from the beginning."

The couple settled into the chairs in front of Jack's desk. Stan leaned forward, becoming serious. He cleared his throat and began.

"Frankie, Bunny, Bix, and I are from New York City." Jack eased behind his desk and withdrew a pad and pen from the top drawer. He nodded at Stan to continue. "I own a construction company. We do pretty well." He grinned, glancing at Bix. "But Frankie had his ups and downs. He started as an agent for musicians in the city, but he got caught up with the wrong people. He slipped in and out of trouble all the time."

"In trouble with the law?" Jack inquired.

"With the law, with clients, with anyone who thought he had crossed them, and there's enough of those," Stan responded.

"What exactly was he doing to provoke the kind of animosity that could lead to murder?"

"Bix and I always tried to stay out of it. I don't know everything he was into, but I guess he was in pretty deep. I'm thinking he may have been cheating some of these musicians. Money or bad contracts, I'm not sure. Bunny would come by the house upset, and we'd try to help, but Frankie wouldn't, or couldn't, change. Sometimes, when things got hot for him in New York, Frankie would go to Pittsburgh or Chicago until things cooled off. Bunny would stay with us or friends in the city, but when Frankie came back, they always got back together. I think there was real love between them, despite everything."

"Have you talked to Bunny?"

"We can't get 'hold of her. She must be staying with friends, but I'll find her. She's going to be really, really hurt by this."

"Why would he come here to New Orleans?" Jack inquired. "Was this a usual stop for him?"

"Not that I know of, but Bunny called and said he'd taken off again and had mentioned New Orleans. He was gone a lot longer than usual, and he was always home for the holidays, so I began to get worried. Bunny told me something else, too." He glanced at Bix and continued. "She thought he might talk to the authorities. Name some names if things got really hot, which could happen with Frankie. He's come close before. It would sure make some people mad. That's when we decided to come down here. We saw the notice in the paper yesterday about the body that was found. We took a chance and went to the cops. Sure enough, it was Frankie. I talked to one of the cops and he gave me your card.

"Frankie never spoke of knowing anyone here in New Orleans?" Jack asked.

"Never. Look, I know it's a needle in a haystack, but I'd really like to know what happened to my brother, and I prefer you to the police. I can pay you real well." He reached into his jacket pocket and brought out a creased photograph. He handed it to Jack. It was a picture of Stan, Bix, and Frankie, along with a short blonde woman.

"That's Bunny, Frankie's wife." Jack took a long look at the photo. He felt like he was already working the case by helping Lieutenant O'Connor. Now he'd have a paying client, but this could be anything from a random robbery to a long-time vendetta. It wouldn't be easy. He leaned across the desk and shook Stan's hand, agreeing to spend two weeks searching for the killer.

"After that we'll leave it to the police. If you think of anything else, call me. And where can I reach you?"

"We're at the Roosevelt, for as long as it takes." Stan responded.

Bix had remained silent, but now she was the first to rise and turn toward the outer office.

"Mrs. Garver will help you with the paperwork," Jack put in.

Well, Bones had been right. Frankie Gerard of New York City had been the victim. What was Frankie really doing here, and who would gun him down on a city street? Stan never mentioned the drugs that Bones had referred to, but perhaps he didn't know. Jack sat back and hooked his hands behind his head. He'd have to talk to Bones again, but now he wanted to see what more he could learn from Lieutenant O'Connor. He stood and adjusted his jacket, reaching for his hat off the rack. The Gerards had departed, and he smiled at Emily as he walked out the door.

Lita Vendome was in her tiny makeshift dressing room at the back of The Anchorage. Salty had converted a storage room for her, and, although it was small, the minimal space provided adequate room for Lita to prepare for her performances. He had painted the walls a brilliant teal, Lita's favorite color, which gave the space a cheerful feel. Against the length of the wall were racks of colorful gowns, waiting to be chosen by Lita for her next show. At the far end sat a wooden dressing table with a huge mirror. The table top was covered with bottles of the singer's lotions and fragrances.

    Lita sat looking into the mirror, examining her face, anticipating the appearance of lines surrounding her eyes. Despite the chaos of bottles on the dressing table, Lita located her usual face cream and began applying it vigorously to her forehead. She sighed and put the bottle down.

    The afternoon's events were weighing on her. She was shocked when she learned Frankie Gerard had been murdered, but she hardly knew the man. He had been in the bar every night for a week, so why did Salty tell Jack he didn't recognize the man in the photo? She went along with him, as had Nettie, but what would Salty have to hide?

She couldn't believe he could be involved in anything like murder. He could be jealous at times, but never violent, despite his sometimes-gruff demeanor. He probably just didn't want any scandal to be associated with The Anchorage. Better not to invite problems. After all, they had nothing to do with the man's demise. Yes, that must be it, she convinced herself with minimal difficulty. She smiled as she continued her ritual, applying the face cream with renewed vigor.

9

When Jack entered Kevin O'Connor's office, he found the Lieutenant seated at his desk up to his elbows in case files and attempting to finish an oyster po' boy.

"Well," he looked up. "Seems we've got a positive ID on our victim."

"And I've got a new client," Jack retorted.

"I thought as much. He seemed pretty anxious, so I sent him over to you. And, once again, I've relied on my friends in the department in New York. They sent this over the wire."

O'Connor shuffled through the paper on his desk and handed Jack a single thin sheet. "Looks like Frankie had his hands in a lot. Misdemeanors, some cases dismissed. Nothing seemed to stick." The Lieutenant smiled. "Oh, I had them take a look at Stan Gerard as well. His company is pretty well known, but he came up clean as far as we know. I think it's going to be a tough one for both of us." He went back to work on the po' boy.

"Thanks," Jack laughed. They agreed to share any further information and Jack returned to his car, driving to Rampart Street to revisit Bones at the music club.

The club was busy, and Bones was delivering a round of drinks to a nearby table as Jack entered. He cleared a place at the bar and Jack took a seat.

"I came clean to Aloha about Frankie. She's okay with it." Bones reached for a beer in the cooler, but Jack waved him off.

"It turns out you were right. His brother identified him, and then hired me to find the killer."

Bones rolled his eyes. "Good luck with that. If I hear anything I'll call you, but it doesn't seem likely. People talk though. I'll keep my eyes and ears open."

"Sure you don't remember anything else about him from your time in New York?" Jack asked.

Bones held his lips together and shook his head. "I think I've told you all I can think of."

Jack rose to leave, opening the door and taking a deep breath of the cool air. He hoped he hadn't taken on something too big to handle.

He walked the two blocks to where Bones and Aloha had found the body. He knelt and gave the scene a thorough inspection. The area had been cleaned after the forensics team had completed their work, and although some stains had not been entirely washed away, Jack found nothing useful to his investigation.

He stood up, pushing his hat back on his head. He turned back down Rampart to his car and, ultimately, to the office.

10

"Oh, here he is now." Emily was on her desk phone as Jack swept into the outer office. She pointed to the phone and mouthed "Nettie Myles" to him. He nodded on the way to his desk. "I'm putting you right through, Mrs. Myles." Emily flicked a switch and hung up the receiver.

"Nettie, what can I do for you?"

"Hey, Jack. I wasn't sure I should call, but it's been eatin' at me since you were at The Anchorage. That man in the picture you showed us. I don't know why Salty said he'd never seen him. I've been at the bar a lot this past week helping Lita with some new music, and that man was in every night. He talked a lot to Lita. I figured he was just a fan, so when Lita went along with Salty, so did I. But it made me stop and think. It sure did, Jack. Salty's as gentle as a bear cub, but you know how he feels about Lita. He'd rather chew rusty nails than let something happen to her, and if he thought she was involved somehow with that man, could he have…" Her voice trailed off.

"Hold on, Nettie. You're getting ahead of yourself." Jack put in. "As much as he adores Lita, I don't think Salty would hurt anyone. Think of all the guys that come to see her perform. He's always been able to restrain himself."

Nettie was silent for a moment, then spoke slowly. "I guess you're right, Jack. Lita's my best friend and I just couldn't bear to see her involved in something like that."

That's probably what Salty thought, too. They had nothing to do with the man's death, so why even acknowledge that they knew him? He kept it simple to avoid any more questions. "If you still have doubts, I'll look into it. But don't worry, I'm sure it's nothing."

He hung up after reassuring Nettie, but he hadn't reassured himself. Salty's behavior was unusual and could even be considered suspicious, and Nettie's call was welcome in a case with so few strands of information to go on.

11

Bix Gerard's frustration was growing. She sat back in the overstuffed armchair in the hotel room, her tired feet propped up conveniently on the matching footstool. What were they supposed to do now, she thought, just sit here and wait? Stan had insisted on hiring that detective in an attempt to thread a delicate needle, but that could bring the persistent detective way too close. If he poked a little too deep into things, it all could really unravel for her and Stan.

      And why bring him in at all? She closed her eyes. Frankie was dead and gone; he wasn't coming back, so what difference could it make? It didn't make sense to draw attention to themselves. They needed to get back to New York as soon as possible. As soon as they could locate her sister, Bunny could take it from there. She was determined to convince Stan to let it go. To return to the city. She knew she could do it; she always did. She would chip away at his resolve until he saw things her way.

She heard the key turn in the door lock as Stan returned, newly purchased pack of cigarettes in hand. She sat up straight and forced a smile. Now was a good time to start.

12

Jack drove down the narrow drive at Velma's boarding house, pulling up in front of the door to his rented rooms. He walked to the front of the house where Velma sat on a porch swing moving slowly back and forth.

"Jack, you doin' alright?" She looked small, curled up on the swing in her floral house dress. Both of her sons had returned to their military bases and her husband was back on the road, so she was glad for Jack's company.

"Got another case, Velma. Looks like a tough one." Jack pulled off his suit jacket, and, rolling up his shirt sleeves, took a seat on the uppermost porch step.

"You always got something going on. I know that, Jack."

"That's a good thing, Velma. A good thing." They both laughed.

The noise emanating from an ancient Ford rounding the corner stifled their conversation. The car stopped in front of the house, and a smiling face leaned out of the driver's window.

"Hello, Miss Velma and Jack Dawson. Haven't seen either of you two for a while now.

The door of the rusty sedan opened and out stepped Rex Charbonne. He walked to the porch and took a seat next to Jack on the step. Rex was a well-known local entrepreneur who sold everything from liquor and cigarettes to men's cologne from the trunk of his car. No one seemed to ever inquire as to the source of any of the available items, and if the police were inclined to request a copy of his vendor's license, they hadn't put forth the effort.

"How's business, Rex?"

"This is my time of year, Jack. I'm all over town around the holidays. I couldn't keep the Lucky Strikes in stock on New Year's." Rex grinned. He leaned back against the porch railing. He wore a loose cotton shirt and baggy trousers whose cuffs draped over his two-toned shoes. His battered straw pork pie sat so far back on his head it resembled a halo.

Velma opened the screen door and popped into the house, returning in a few moments with two bottles of grape Nehi which she handed to Jack and Rex.

Jack took the opportunity to pull the picture Stan had given him out of his jacket pocket. Rex took a large gulp of his soda as he reached for the photo. He studied the picture for a long time, then shook his head as he enjoyed another swig from the bottle.

"That's the man that was killed on Rampart. I saw his picture in the paper." He pointed to Frankie with his middle finger. "But nope, I don't remember seeing any of them."

Jack nodded. "Anything seem out of the ordinary or unusual on New Year's Eve?" He knew Rex, if anybody, was the eyes and ears of the city.

Rex threw back his head and laughed, "Unusual? On New Year's Eve? In New Orleans? You know everything's unusual in New Orleans, not just on New Year's." He laughed again and finished the last of his Nehi.

"One thing I do remember, though, because it looked kinda' funny." He looked at Jack. "I was turning off Royal Street onto Canal and who do I see moving down Canal at a real clip? Old Salty Evans from down at The Anchorage. I never saw Salty move so fast, and I wondered why he wasn't at his bar. It must have been packed on New Year's Eve."

Jack sat up straight. "What time was that?

"Oh, about nine or ten, I guess."

"Was he headed toward Rampart?"

"In that direction, yeah, but I drove on. Didn't see him again."

Jack sat back again. Now, this was some interesting information that might lead to something. His thoughts were interrupted by Velma.

"I got red beans and rice on the stove. You two coming?"

Jack had forgotten how hungry he was, so he rose and followed Velma and Rex into the kitchen.

13

Jack donned a favorite suit and fedora as he left Velma's the following morning. He knew he had to revisit Salty and Lita after his conversations with both Nettie and Rex. He didn't want to believe Salty could be involved in the murder, but this was a lead that had to be explored. He pointed the sedan across Canal and onto St. Charles, parking on a side street behind The Anchorage. The back door of the bar was open, Salty trying to dissipate the heat from the pots on the stove in the tiny kitchen, leaving only the screen door closed. Jack could see Salty's shadow as he bustled about, adjusting the burners on the stove, then turning to the radio that sat on a countertop. He rotated the control knob through a cacophony of voices and melodies, finally settling on the cool sounds emanating from Benny Goodman's clarinet. Salty jerked his head around when Jack knocked on the screen door frame.

"Jack," he squinted. "You startled me."

"Sorry, Salty. Just want to ask you a few more questions about that fellow they found on Rampart."

"I don't know what more I can tell you. Like I said, I never saw the guy." Salty fidgeted with his apron strings.

"I've heard he stopped in the bar to see Lita more than once. And you were seen on Canal Street New Year's Eve when you should have been here at the club. Come on Salty, what's really going on?"

Salty turned to open a pantry cupboard, moving aside bags of flour and jars of spices. He swung around and confronted Jack, gripping an ancient, rusted pistol.

"I didn't kill that guy, Jack."

"And you're not going to kill me, either. That thing hasn't been fired in years."

Salty bit his lip while looking down at the gun, slowly putting it down on the countertop. He eased himself into a chair at a small table against the wall near the stove. He rubbed his face, then rested his head in his hands as he leaned on the table.

"The guy started coming in the bar about a week or so ago. At first, he just watched Lita's show. Then he hung around to talk to her. He spent more and more time with Lita, and I guess I got a little suspicious."

"Jealous, you mean."

"Yeah, you know. I should have spoken to Lita right then, but I didn't." He shrugged. "Anyway, he showed up again on New Year's Eve and I saw him walk out with Lita after her first set. I wanted to go after them, but by the time I got our bartender, Buddy, I had lost them. A few minutes later, I see the guy running past the front window, so I went out after him." He gave

Jack a sheepish look. "I just wanted to ask him what he wanted with Lita, but he was moving pretty fast. I couldn't keep up. I lost him on Canal Street."

"Was he headed toward Rampart?"

Salty nodded affirmatively. "I never saw him again. When I got back to the bar, Lita was in her second set, so I let it go for the rest of the night. I tried not to think about it until you showed up with that picture. I didn't want to make things any more complicated, so I told you I hadn't seen him before. Lita and I talked about it later. I guess you'll need to talk to her. She's upstairs." He rolled his eyes upwards indicating Lita's second-floor apartment.

14

Jack ascended the steep, narrow staircase that separated the kitchen and the bar. Lita responded to his knock almost immediately. She greeted Jack in a button-down blouse with a lace collar, a pair of sturdy trousers, and flat shoes. Her face, devoid of makeup, still emitted a radiant glow. She led him through the living room area into a small kitchen where she poured them both a cup of coffee.

    He sat at the kitchen table facing the living room, which was open and airy, the furniture modern and comfortable. Framed photographs and ceramic figurines crowded a shelf along the far wall while a large radio and a phonograph competed for space underneath a picture window. The homey rooms seem to reveal a more casual Lita that somehow felt more real than the gown-clad singer that reveled in the spotlight.

    The radio was tuned to the same broadcast as Salty's, and she turned down the volume before returning to the kitchen. She sat opposite Jack at the table and began to speak.

"I first met Frank Gerard years ago while I was performing in New York. All the musicians knew him. He had quite a reputation. Not a good one, I can assure you."

"Bones Barnett told me all about it." Jack responded.

Lita nodded, wrapped her hand around her coffee cup, and continued.

"Well, we really never traveled in the same circles, and I never gave him a second thought. I moved here with my late husband, and I've been singing here at Salty's now for years. So, I was really surprised to see Frankie at the bar this past week. He took the table near the stage, and I recognized him right away. No one could forget those electric eyes."

Jack smiled.

"He stayed around after the show. He said he recognized me from my picture out front and wanted to say hello. He was alone in New Orleans, and it was good to see a familiar face. He came in every night after that, always at the same table. There was something sad or lost about him. I don't know. So, when he asked if we could go somewhere to talk on New Year's Eve, I agreed. After my first set, we went down the street to that diner near Poydras Street. He said he'd been worried that someone was after him, but he wouldn't tell me who or why. I told him to go to the police, but he refused. That's when I gave him your card. He put it in his pocket without even looking at it. He didn't say much more, but he became upset when he saw a man pass by our table. A second later, Frankie ran out of the diner. I never saw him again."

"Had you ever seen the other man before? What did he look like?"

"I never saw him before, or since. He was odd-looking, though. He wore a bright plaid suit in reds and yellows. He drew his hat down, so I didn't get a good look at his face. I remember wondering why someone would wear such a loud suit if they didn't want to be noticed by the person they were following."

"Maybe he wanted to be seen. To put a scare into Frankie."

"Well, it sure worked. I never saw anyone move as fast as Frankie did that night." She flashed a wry smile. "I just went back to the bar and began my second set. I didn't know that Salty had gone after him until much later." She got up and refilled both of their coffees. Jack took a sip as Lita went on.

"When you came in with that picture, I was shocked that Frankie was dead. When Salty denied having ever seen him, I went along with it. I figured he had a good reason; he's such an honest guy." She smiled again. "But I was worried about Salty. I just can't believe he'd have anything to do with Frankie's death." Her face grew tight, her brow furrowed.

"Neither can I," Jack said as she relaxed slightly. He pulled out the photo that Stan had given him, but she only recognized Frankie.

Jack thanked her. She closed the door behind him as he eased down the narrow staircase. He believed Salty and Lita. At least he didn't want to believe they were involved. The man in the loud suit. Now here was a lead. Or so he hoped.

15

Jack arrived at the office to find Emily busily organizing files and scribbling on note cards in an effort to keep Jack abreast of the latest happenings in the office. She was taking a long weekend off to visit her sister in Biloxi and, in her meticulous fashion, was determined to leave everything in perfect order. By the time she had covered her typewriter, adjusted her hat, and bid goodbye to Jack, she was confident she had done just that.

Jack sat at his desk in the inner office, still thinking about the man in the plaid suit. The possibly definitive lead would be tough to pursue. It looked like trouble had followed Frankie here from New York, which would make finding any answers more difficult.

The ringing telephone startled him out of his thoughts, although he was glad to hear Kevin O'Connor's voice on the line. Jack filled him in on what Lita and Salty had told him. The Lieutenant agreed that Salty was an unlikely suspect, but he couldn't rule him out entirely.

"I'll send someone over to talk to Lita, see if she can remember anything more about your flashy mystery man, but I've got something you might find interesting. While we've been checking hotels to find out where Frank Gerard was staying, we came across a curious name on the roster at a rooming house in the Marigny. A Beatrice Bixby checked in three days before New Year's. Sounded enough like your client to catch my eye. Might be nothing, but I thought I'd let you look into it."

"Give me the address. I'll take a photo over there to see if anyone can identify her."

They agreed to keep in contact with any information relevant to their mutual investigations, and Jack rang off.

Jack rubbed the back of his neck. Here was a new twist. If Beatrice Bixby was Bix Gerard, what was she doing in New Orleans three days earlier than she had told him? And where was Stan?

Jack grabbed his hat, headed to an address in the Marigny.

16

Jack drove down the tiny street off Esplanade Avenue past a row of dilapidated homes, at the end of which sat the rooming house. The house, itself a victim of neglect, sat back from the road behind several feet of unmanicured lawn. The peeling paint contributed to a general sense of sadness surrounding the place, and the day's gray sky added to its forlorn appearance. If the contribution of flowerpots with colorful red geraniums placed strategically on the wraparound porch was an attempt to provide cheerfulness to the depressing scene, it definitely failed.

  An old wooden sign attached to the front of the house advertised rooms for rent, and a vacancy sign below it came as no surprise. To the rear of the house in an equal state of disrepair was a garage-like building, squat and square, in front of which a child's bicycle lay on its side in a muddy puddle.

  It was surely not the type of place anyone would expect to find Stan or Bix Gerard, Jack thought as he pushed the front door. It opened into a small living room that, although sparsely furnished, was clean and orderly in comparison to the outside of the house. An improvised office had been made from a converted closet, complete with a Dutch door. A woman leaned out of the top half, addressing Jack as he entered.

"I've got one room available, just at the top of the stairs. No hot plate, no pets. Long-term or short-term..."

She attempted to continue, but Jack stopped her by raising a hand. He informed her of the reason for his visit, retrieved the picture Stan had given him, and handed it to her. She gathered her thick graying hair and pulled it back into a hair band before reaching for the photo. Her hands were rough, her nails uneven, and she held the picture close to her face as she studied it.

"Oh yeah, that's Miss Bixby. She was here earlier in the week." She didn't recognize anyone else, she said. "Miss Bixby wasn't particularly friendly, but she paid in advance and didn't cause any trouble." She smiled at Jack, enjoying the opportunity for conversation.

"And she insisted on the place out back." She nodded toward the rear of the house. "We've got one room off the garage. Folks like it. It's very private." She smiled again as she reached for a pack of cigarettes on the desk behind her.

Jack started to speak when the front door flew open. A young boy ran in, approaching the office. "Hey, Ma..." He drew up short when he saw Jack. He looked slowly up and down at the detective. "Are you a cop or something?"

The boy had close-cropped auburn hair, a striped t-shirt, and a pair of muddy dungarees. The probable owner of the bicycle in the yard, Jack surmised.

"No, I'm not a cop."

The woman leaned over the half door. "William, mind your manners."

"Uh-oh. She only calls me William when she means business." He reached up and grabbed the picture off the door counter. "That's the lady that stayed in the back." He pointed to Bix. "That's the man too." He indicated Stan with a bandaged finger.

"You saw that man here?" Jack nodded at Stan's image in the picture.

"Yep, he was back there with her. I see everything that's going on around here."

"William!" His mother raised her voice, which caused William to make an escape out the front door. She took a deep breath, noticing the muddy footprints on the living room floor. "Kids," was all she said as she traded the unlit cigarette for a mop from inside the office.

Jack walked back to his car. As light rain began, it softened the mud and he cursed to himself as it covered his shoes while he navigated the pathway. He drove off, wondering what Stan and Bix had been doing here, what were they hiding? He wanted to talk with them to find out if they knew anything about the man in the plaid suit, but he'd keep his knowledge of their stay at the rooming house to himself. He hated the idea of having to investigate his own clients, but that may be exactly what he would have to do.

17

Stan Gerard nursed a drink at a table in the hotel bar. He took a sip, then stubbed out another Lucky Strike in the nearly full ashtray. Where was that waitress? He wanted, no, he needed another scotch and water.
He had spoken to the detective. He didn't expect much progress in such a short time, and there didn't seem to be any. The detective asked about a man who had frightened Frankie. A flashy stranger that appeared to be following him, but heck, that could be anyone. It did seem to prove one thing, though: someone knew Frankie was here and had come after him. Frankie might have had trouble with a local, but not enough to get him killed. It had to be someone from New York. If what Bunny had told him was true, that Frankie was going to talk, a lot of people would do what it takes to shut him up.

    He finished the last of his scotch, weighing his options. Bunny was in town. He talked to her this morning. He was beginning to think Bix was right; they should go back to New York and let Bunny take it from here. They could pay off the detective and go home, back to familiar territory. He had a lot to lose, and he had taken a chance by hiring the detective in the first place. He wanted to know the truth, but it might just be too big a risk.

　　He got up, threw a few dollars on the table, and left the bar.

18

Jack was back in the office going through some paperwork Emily had left for him. He had spoken to Lieutenant O'Connor, but still felt uncertain about how to proceed with an investigation of his own clients. The phone rang as he opened a file folder, and the voice, when he answered, was so soft and childlike he thought it was a prank.

"Is this Mr. Dawson?"

"Yes."

"I need to speak with you. It's important."

"Does your mother know you're playing on the telephone?" Jack laughed.

"Oh no, Mr. Dawson. This is Bunny Gerard. Stan said he'd hired you."

Jack sat up. "I'm sorry, Mrs. Gerard."

"It's okay. It happens all the time."

"I mean, I'm sorry about your husband. What can I do for you?"

"I just wanted to tell you, well, my brother-in-law isn't who he seems to be. He and Frankie weren't as close as he likes to make everyone believe. In fact, they were at odds most of the time. I think I made a mistake. I told Stan that Frankie was coming here. I hope he didn't do anything terrible." He heard her sobbing, but she immediately composed herself. "I have to go now. I just wanted to tell you."

"Where can I reach you?"

"Oh, I'll be so busy making the arrangements for Frankie I'll have to get in touch with you."

She hung up. The mysterious call left Jack with a head full of unanswered questions. Was the motive for Frankie's death more sinister than he had anticipated? If Stan and Bix were involved, why had they hired him? He grabbed his hat as he headed toward the outer office when he was stopped by the ringing telephone. This time it was the voice of Kevin O'Connor on the line.

"Jack, meet me at The Anchorage. Someone's taken a shot at Lita Vendome."

19

Jack pulled up to The Anchorage where patrol cars had cornered off the back entrance. He was directed to Lita's upstairs apartment. He once again navigated the narrow staircase and entered to find Lita, Salty, and Lieutenant O'Connor seated in the living room. They looked up as Lita was beginning to describe the afternoon's events. The Lieutenant urged her to continue.

"Well, I had gone through the kitchen and out the back door. I often do that to get some fresh air, usually between sets when the club gets hot and smoky. Today I went out early. Salty had been cooking for tonight's crowd and the heat from the kitchen was stifling. I stood out there for a few minutes. It was cool and damp, but it felt good. When the mist began to turn into actual rain, I turned to go back inside. I had just reached to open the screen when I heard the shot. It came right past me, close enough to startle me. I threw open the door and hurried inside."

"You didn't see anyone?" the Lieutenant asked.

"No one. It was gray and a little foggy. I didn't see anyone back there at all."

"Can you think of anyone who would think they had a reason to come after you?"

Lita smiled. "I know what you're thinking, Lieutenant. I have a lot of fans but there's no reason to think that one felt provoked into attacking me."

The Lieutenant raised his eyebrows. "How about you?" He turned to Salty. "Anybody with a grudge against you?"

Salty shook his head. "But I'll tell you this. I won't let anything happen to Lita. I'll go after anyone who tries to lay a hand on her." He was obviously agitated, and the Lieutenant attempted to calm him.

"Salty, let us handle it. You don't want to get yourself into trouble. What would happen if you weren't here?"

Salty shook his head.

"He's right, Salty," Lita said. "I'm fine and it's going to be all right. The Lieutenant is posting a guard, and they'll get it all sorted out." Lita was remarkably calm, and her steadiness seemed to soothe the upset bar owner.

Lieutenant O'Connor asked a few more questions, then got up to leave. Lita went into the kitchen and Jack followed right behind.

"Lita." She turned. "Are you sure Frankie didn't say something, anything, that someone wouldn't want you to know?"

She shook her head. "Everything I told you the other day was true. Frankie was afraid that someone was after him, and he ran away when he saw that man, but he never told me what it was about."

"That shot might have been a warning for you to keep quiet," Jack stated.

"But I don't know anything."

"The shooter might think you do."

"You're right that it might have been a warning. It was foggy out, but I was a wide-open target. Even a fair shot could have taken me out with no trouble if they wanted to."

Jack had to agree, and he rubbed his chin as Salty came in from the living room.

"I wasn't kidding out there, Jack. I won't let anything happen to Lita. Anybody comes after her, they're going to pay."

"Just keep her away from the back door. Keep an eye on her. The police will be around," Jack responded.

"Think we should cancel the show tonight?"

"No," Lita jumped in. "I'm going on as usual. This won't stop me."

Her voice was strong and determined, and Salty acquiesced, heading down the staircase to finish preparing for the evening.

Jack followed, deep in thought. This added another new twist to everything. So many pieces to the puzzle, but nothing seemed to connect. He reached the rear entrance, examining the door frame where the forensic team had retrieved the bullet. He rubbed his hand over the splintered wood. He stood back, observing the scene, returned to the car, and drove back across Canal Street and into the Quarter.

20

Jack had a restless night and spent the morning speaking with Kevin O'Connor once again. The police had come up empty on the flashy dresser, and O'Connor's associates in New York had taken a closer look at the Gerards, but nothing had come back yet. The night had passed with no disturbances at The Anchorage, which Jack was relieved to hear.

He stopped at Bones's music club to fill Bones and Aloha in on the status of the case and to partake in another one of Aloha's lunches. The couple had heard about Lita and were concerned that someone from the music community had been targeted.

"I can't help but think the shot at Lita and the Gerard murder are connected. Someone thinks Lita knows something," Jack mused.

"You think she does?" Bones asked.

"I think she told me everything Frankie told her. Lita wouldn't hold anything back."

Bones nodded. Jack reached into his pocket for coins for the jukebox, emptying the contents on the bar in a futile search for nickels. Aloha swept out of the kitchen, placing a plate in front of Jack.

"Gotta keep your strength up," she smiled. She looked down at the business cards and matchbooks he had placed on the bar. She picked up the photograph that had been pulled out as well. It was the picture Stan had given him. She studied it for a few moments.

"Oh, I've seen her before," she said.

"This one?" Jack pointed at Bix.

"No, the one on the left," indicating Bunny.

"When did you see her?" Jack's voice quickened.

"On New Year's Eve. I remember because she was alone. She ordered a bitter lemon, but when I turned back around, she was gone."

"Are you sure it was New Year's? It couldn't have been later in the week?"

"I'm sure."

"And you're sure it was this woman?"

"Yeah, she kind of stood out. A looker with expensive clothes. Her voice was so soft I had to ask her twice for her order."

It was Bunny all right, thought Jack, but that meant she had been in New Orleans before Frankie had been killed. It wasn't just Stan and Bix harboring secrets; now Bunny was hiding the truth about being here. Another layer, another complication.

21

Time was running out, thought Bix Gerard. It was obviously time to return to New York. Eventually someone would be arrested for the murder and that would be the end of it. Hopefully...

They had a business to run. And besides, she needed the safety and familiarity of home. She craved the sense of being in control and she didn't feel that here.

She would talk to Stan again. He was getting restless himself. They would go immediately to the detective's office, pay him for his trouble, and head north. It was time.

22

Bunny Gerard couldn't focus. Everything was hazy. She was wandering in the French Quarter, peering into shop windows. She liked it here in this city. It had a grittiness that reminded her of New York, and a connection to its past that every city should have. But that didn't matter now. She had a purpose, a mission, and she had to try to concentrate.

Frankie was gone; that was real, no matter what else happened. Focusing on what was real was becoming increasingly difficult. It was as if every time she attempted to reach out and grasp the reality, it would move farther away, teasingly, then vanish, leaving her lost and confused.

She moved more rapidly past the storefronts, determined to concentrate. Focus, focus, she told herself. There was more to be done.

23

Jack tried to tie together the threads. Piece together the thin slivers of information he had learned so far. He was so deep in thought as he walked to his car behind Bones' club that he didn't notice the tall figure coming up behind him. He felt a dull stab in his side, and he had no reason to doubt it was the barrel of a gun.

"To the gray sedan, parked on the street." The gunman bumped the barrel twice more into Jack's side. Jack followed the man's direction. He'd been carrying his pistol regularly since a case last year, but he had no opportunity to retrieve it, and a shootout on the street would certainly not yield a favorable outcome for either of them.

"The driver's side. Slide over," the man ordered. Jack obeyed, and even though he contemplated an escape attempt through the passenger door, it would be an uncomfortably painful option.

To Jack's surprise, the driver turned the car back into the Quarter where the traffic would move slowly, as opposed to heading out of town.

"Just want to have a little talk with you," the driver chuckled.

"Talk? About what?" Out of the corner of his eye, Jack could see the expensive leather shoes pressing the gas pedal and the clutch; and the gold silk socks almost covered by copper-colored trouser legs. He knew who he was dealing with, but not what the stranger wanted.

"It's about who you're working for. Stan Gerard. He's your client, isn't he?" the stranger stated.

"I'm looking into the death of his brother, Frankie."

"That's what I heard but let me give you a warning. Stan's no angel."

"You're not the first person to tell me that," Jack stated. "You think Stan may have some involvement in what happened to Frankie?"

"Let's just say it's more than possible."

They were crossing Toulouse Street heading deeper into the Quarter. The traffic was creeping, barely moving. The driver was steering clumsily, keeping a hand on the steering wheel and changing gears as he attempted to keep his pistol aimed at Jack.

"What's your interest in all this?" Jack inquired.

"What's your connection to Frankie and Stan?"

"Me?" The man laughed. "I sorta got a client myself." He laughed again. "I got a reason to see things go a certain way. That's where we can work together. We can make sure Stan gets what's coming to him."

"You want me to set up my client for the murder of his brother; a murder he may not have committed?" asked Jack.

The car lurched to the right and turned, heading back toward Canal Street, but was trapped once again in crawling traffic.

"You don't have to set up anybody, just help me put him where he belongs. There's money in it for you. More than Stan Gerard will pay you." The timbre of the man's voice was rising. Jack could sense the anger. He took a glance at the driver; his ruddy complexion getting redder under his fedora.

"Look straight ahead," the man motioned to Jack with the pistol. "If you don't want to cooperate, I think I can help you change your mind." He looked down at his hand holding the gun.

Jack weighed his limited options. Attempting to grab the gun or the steering wheel could be disastrous. They continued inching along, wedged between cars in front and back. They pulled up beside a mule cart overloaded with fruits and vegetables. The passenger door had remained unlocked, and Jack took a chance. He threw open the car door, slamming it into the side of the cart, unleashing an avalanche of melons and mirlitons. He dashed under the cart, rolling to the far side as the startled mule reared. The cart driver managed to keep the animal from running off, avoiding a further catastrophe. Jack ducked into a souvenir shop, keeping an eye on the location of his abductor's car. The car remained trapped between the slow-moving vehicles and Jack was easily able to escape into a throng of tourists, but not before attaining the number on the car's New York license plate.

    Jack wiped off his dirtied suit, noticing, with a frown, a tear on the knee of his trousers.

24

Jack contacted Kevin O'Connor about the New York plate, and the return call was almost immediate. The car belonged to Johnny Florentino, a small-time hoodlum with crime family connections. His connection to Stan and Frankie Gerard was unknown.

Certainly, thought Jack, Frankie would have known a lot of shady types in his line of work, but what about Stan? Why was Johnny so anxious to put Stan out of commission? Bunny had expressed the same sentiment about her brother-in-law, but why?

He needed to confront Stan and Bix. It was time for them to come clean.

25

Jack didn't have to go far to come face to face with both Stan and Bix. He rose to answer a knock at his office door, and the couple entered, Stan gripping his hat in his hands, Bix guarded in her quiet stoicism. They moved to Jack's desk and Stan cleared his throat to announce their departure from New Orleans.

"Of course, we'll pay you for your time, but Bunny is here now and it's time for us to go back to New York. We can't be away from our business for too long and, well, whomever took out Frankie, it'll come to light sooner or later."

Jack had to think fast. He needed to keep the couple in town at least a little while longer to find out what they were up to, what part they played in the murder. He saw that Stan had taken notice of his scraped knuckles from his dive under the vegetable cart.

"I had a bit of a run in with our flashy mystery man. He seems to think that you're involved somehow."

Stan fumbled with his hat. "I just wanted to find out what happened to Frankie. Who is the mystery guy anyway?"

"We found out he's a small-time thug out of New York."

Stan rubbed his chin. "Somebody gunning after Frankie, I suppose. I'm not surprised."

"The man told me he had a client. Do you know what that might mean or who that could be?"

Stan shook his head. "Frankie led a complicated life. He knew a lot of people, and not always the best people. I'm sure he made enemies. I mean, it could be anybody."

Stan was cut short by the sound of the inner office door being pushed open. A diminutive figure stood in the doorway, hesitated, then strode with conviction to Jack's desk.

"Bunny." It was all Stan could say.

They stood facing each other like opponents in a boxing ring, with Jack in the center, a potential referee. So, this was Bunny, thought Jack. The tiny woman wore a form-fitted cream silk dress accented with blue lace; and where her sister Bix was all rough edges, Bunny eluded an air of both softness and animal sexuality, with a figure that stayed out all night, but a face that went to church on Sunday. Her blonde hair floated around her face, but her eyes appeared glazed and unfocused. She threw her head back with a disturbing laugh.

"I followed you two here." She looked from Stan to Bix. Her parted crimson lips revealed a pair of predominant front teeth, making the moniker Bunny seem both appropriate and somehow endearing. She continued in her off-putting, childish voice.

"I knew when I told you that Frankie was going to the authorities that you would follow him down here. If you thought your empire was going to crumble, you'd be the first one to bring him down." She giggled. "Do you really think Frankie would talk? With all he had to lose?" She smiled with a misplaced sense of pride. "I started that rumor. My mistake was not waiting for you to take care of Frankie, but I couldn't wait. I couldn't give you the satisfaction."

Jack stared directly at her. "It was you..."

26

Emily had spent a wonderful long weekend in Biloxi. She saw her niece's new baby and caught up with her sister, and, if the cooler weather had prohibited many outdoor activities, good food and games of cards at the dinner table made the time enjoyable for everyone. In good spirits, she and her husband made good time on the drive home, and she decided to stop in at the office to look in on Jack and, ever efficient, check up on his secretarial abilities.

She padded up the stairs to the office. She found the outer door open, and she heard voices as she entered. She didn't hear Jack, just a man's voice and a woman speaking in an unusually high pitch. She hesitated. Something wasn't right and, trusting her instinct, she turned silently and hurried back down the staircase. Reaching the ground floor, she turned into the neighboring muffuletta shop. She reached into her bag for her coin purse as she rushed to the pay phone in the rear of the store. Her fingers trembled as she dropped the change into the slots and placed her call.

27

"Yes, it was me." Bunny giggled again. It was becoming increasingly evident she was irrational. "You see, I knew you'd go after Frankie if you thought he was going to bring you down. If you didn't have the guts to kill your own brother, I could make it look like you did. It was Johnny's idea at first, but he pushed too hard, scaring Frankie and coming after you, detective." She smiled, her eyes wild. "Now Stan, you're going to lose it all anyway."

She reached into her delicate handbag and pulled out a tiny revolver. She pointed it at Stan. She glanced at Bix. "Sorry, sis."

"You're crazy." Stan was sweating. He rushed toward the window behind Jack's desk, threw it open, and attempted to climb out. His girth made a quick exit impossible, and he struggled, half in and half out, like a scene from a Keystone comedy. In his rush to the window, he had pushed Bix up against the office wall and now, as she recovered her balance, she looked back and forth between Stan and Bunny in an attempt to prioritize her loyalties. After a few moments, she determinedly edged toward the office door.

Bunny fired a shot at the window just as Jack grabbed her arm, and the bullet lodged itself in the window frame as Stan finally extricated himself and reached the metal stairs of the fire escape. He started down but was trapped by the prompt arrival of a patrol car at the base of the stairs.

Jack was still holding Bunny's wrist when Lieutenant O'Connor and a team of policemen pounded up the office stairway and came through the door. Bunny continued laughing as she was handcuffed, her voice disturbingly eerie.

"If you're looking for Johnny, you'll find him at our motel on the highway. I took care of him while he was sleeping. I didn't want to leave a blood stain on any of his fancy suits. Oh, and tell that little songbird how lucky she is. I followed Frankie to that bar for nearly a week. She's a pretty one. Frankie always liked the pretty ones." Her voice got softer, barely audible, but she quickly grinned and spoke loudly again. "I just wanted to give her a scare." She laughed as she was led out, followed by Bix with a uniformed officer. Stan had been escorted to the patrol car and now sat frowning in the backseat.

Lieutenant O'Connor was headed out of the office. "You've got a pretty sharp secretary, Jack. She put in the call."

Jack nodded as he followed the lieutenant down the stairs.

28

Jack had given his statement, as had the others, and he'd been able to garner additional information to put the puzzle pieces together. It seemed Bunny and her new boyfriend Johnny had started the rumor about Frankie talking to the authorities.

Stan was the Kingpin behind Frankie's drug activity; all being laundered by the construction company. They thought if they told Stan that Frankie was headed here, he would follow, and if he didn't take Frankie out himself to shut him up, he could easily be framed for it. Bunny always thought Stan was responsible for most of Frankie's troubles, and she grew to hate Frankie for all he'd put her through. She didn't seem to care one way or another about her sister, Bix, in the end. And when she thought Johnny was about to ruin everything with his actions, she did him in as well.

She's obviously unwell, Jack thought, and Lita was lucky. Bunny was capable of anything.

Jack took a walk to the riverfront. Few ships were in the choppy water, and everything was enveloped in shades of gray. He thought about Bunny, her circumstances, the physical and mental bruising that shaped her and made her capable of her actions. Everyone bores the scars of their past. He himself carried the burden of a troubled childhood. How were some people able to navigate the cruelty and injustice in their worlds while others succumbed to the worst of it?

It grew cooler as a wind blew across the river and mist dampened the air. He turned away from the water, pulling up his coat collar and tugging his hat down on his head. He had been seeing Rosamund Devereaux, and she would be back from Baton Rouge by now, he thought. He'd call her from the office. They both could use a night out.

29

Lita Vendome peered out of her dressing room. The lights were dim except for the ones near the stage where her backup trio was warming up. She looked at the tables surrounding the stage. Minnie and her husband sat at a front-row table; their faces reflected in the glow of candlelight. Nearby, ironically at the table that Frankie had always occupied, sat Jack Dawson, accompanied by an attractive young lady. She looked to her right, straining her neck for a glimpse of Salty's silhouette as he mixed cocktails at the bar.

"I guess I love the guy." She laughed at herself for saying it out loud.

The trio began and a single spotlight circled the microphone, indicating her entrance. She smoothed the folds in her gown and walked out to her audience. As it had always been said, the show would go on.

The End

Made in the USA
Middletown, DE
27 July 2024

58029544R00044